STORIES of DRAGONS and BEASTS

Gayatri Kalra Sehgal is an internationally acclaimed author, an artist and a passionate educationist. She set up a daycare centre and two schools, first as the principal and later as a dean, and carefully designed their academic curricula. In 2013, she innovated and revolutionized a novel way of writing report cards, renaming them as 'Child's Intelligence Profile'.

She regularly conducts interactive seminars and engaging workshops on the National Education Policy 2020 (NEP 2020), child development, learning styles, curriculum design, effective communication, authorpreneurship, emotional well-being during the pandemic, and more, sensitizing educators towards holistic teaching and learning approaches. Her work, including her motivational speeches, is aimed at encouraging awareness and sensitivity, and offering support to parents of differently-abled children.

Her 13 published books are an extensive collection of her unique experiences and her vision to inspire global leaders for tomorrow.

Also by the Author

Greatest Ever Aesop's Fables

Tales of Fairies, Witches and Magic

Become a Mathematician in 21 Days

Become a Brilliant Thinker in 21 Days

Become a Creative Genius in 21 Days

Being a Mathematician: Mastering Secrets of Mental Math

Being a Brilliant Thinker: Mastering Intelligent Thinking Skills

Being a Creative Genius: Mastering Activities That Inspire Creativity

Super Child! Unlocking the Secrets of Working Memory

Winning Strategies for Parents: Helping Your Child Excel at Home and School

STORIES *of* DRAGONS *and* BEASTS

Gayatri Kalra Sehgal

Published by
Rupa Publications India Pvt. Ltd 2023
7/16, Ansari Road, Daryaganj
New Delhi 110002

Sales centres:
Bengaluru Chennai
Hyderabad Jaipur Kathmandu
Kolkata Mumbai Prayagraj

Edition copyright © Rupa Publications India Pvt. Ltd 2023

All rights reserved.
No part of this publication may be reproduced, transmitted, or stored in a retrieval system, in any form or by any means, electronic, mechanical, photocopying, recording or otherwise, without the prior permission of the publisher.

P-ISBN: 978-93-5702-988-9
E-ISBN: 978-93-5702-905-6

First impression 2023

10 9 8 7 6 5 4 3 2 1

Printed in India

This book is sold subject to the condition that it shall not, by way of trade or otherwise, be lent, resold, hired out, or otherwise circulated, without the publisher's prior consent, in any form of binding or cover other than that in which it is published.

To my sons,
Divyamshu and Kuber

Contents

The Dragon of the North   1

The Dragon and His Grandmother   20

The Prince and the Dragon   25

Beauty and the Beast   37

The Dragon's Tail   64

Acknowledgements   80

The Dragon of the North

Very long ago, as old people have told me, there lived a terrible monster, who came out of the North, and laid waste whole tracts of country, devouring both men and beasts; and this monster was so destructive that it was feared that unless help came no living creature would be left on the face of the earth.

It had a body like an ox, and legs like a frog, two short fore-legs, and two long ones behind, and besides that it had a tail like a serpent, ten fathoms in length. When it moved it jumped like a frog, and with every spring it covered half a mile of ground. Fortunately its habit was to remain for several years in the same place, and not to move on till the whole neighbourhood was eaten up.

Nothing could hunt it, because its whole body was covered with scales, which were harder than stone or metal; its two great eyes shone by night, and even by day, like the brightest lamps, and anyone who had the ill luck to look into those eyes became as it were bewitched, and was obliged to rush of his own accord into the monster's jaws. In this way the Dragon was able to feed upon both men and beasts without the least trouble to itself, as it needed not to move from the spot where it was lying. All the neighbouring kings had offered rich rewards to anyone who should be able to destroy the monster, either by force or enchantment, and many had tried their luck, but all had miserably failed.

Once a great forest in which the Dragon lay had been set on fire; the forest was burnt down, but the fire did not do the monster the least harm. However, there was a tradition amongst the wise men of the country that the Dragon might be overcome by the one who possessed King Solomon's signet-ring, upon which a secret writing was engraved. This inscription would enable anyone who was wise enough to interpret it to find out how the Dragon could be destroyed. Only no one knew where the ring was hidden, nor was there any sorcerer or learned man to be found who would be able to explain the inscription.

At last a young man, with a good heart and plenty of courage, set out to search for the ring. He took his way towards the sun-rising, because he knew that all the wisdom of old time comes from the East. After some years, he met with a famous Eastern magician, and asked for his advice in the matter. The magician answered:

'Mortal men have but little wisdom, and can give you no help, but the birds of the air would be better guides to you if you could learn their language. I can help you to understand it if you will stay with me a few days.'

The youth thankfully accepted the magician's offer, and said, 'I cannot now offer you any reward for your kindness, but should my undertaking succeed your trouble shall be richly repaid.'

Then the magician brewed a powerful potion out of nine sorts of herbs which he had gathered himself all alone by moonlight, and he gave the youth nine spoonfuls of it daily for three days, which made him able to understand the language of birds.

At parting, the magician said to him, 'If you ever find Solomon's ring and get possession of it, then come back to me, that I may explain the inscription on the ring to you, for there is no one else in the world who can do this.'

From that time the youth never felt lonely as he walked along; he always had company, because he understood the language of birds; and in this way he learned many things which mere human knowledge could never have taught him. But time went on, and he heard nothing about the ring. It happened one evening, when he was hot and tired with walking, and had sat down under a tree in a forest to eat his supper, that he saw two gaily-plumaged birds, that were strange to him, sitting at the top of the tree talking to one another about him. The first bird said:

'I know that wandering fool under the tree there, who has come so far without finding what he seeks. He is trying to find King Solomon's lost ring.'

The other bird answered, 'He will have to seek help from the Witch-maiden, who will doubtless be able to put him on the right track. If she has not got the ring herself, she knows well enough who has it.'

'But where is he to find the Witch-maiden?' said the first bird. 'She has no settled dwelling, but is here today and gone tomorrow. He might as well try to catch the wind.'

The other replied, 'I do not know, certainly, where she is at present, but in three nights from now she will come to the spring to wash her face, as she does every month when the moon is full, in order that she may never grow old nor wrinkled, but may always keep the bloom of youth.'

'Well,' said the first bird, 'the spring is not far from here. Shall we go and see how it is she does it?'

'Willingly, if you like,' said the other.

The youth immediately resolved to follow the birds to the spring, only two things made him uneasy: first, lest he might be asleep when the birds went, and secondly, lest he might lose sight of them, since he had not wings to carry him along so swiftly. He was too tired to keep awake all night, yet his anxiety prevented him from sleeping soundly, and when with the earliest dawn he looked up to the tree-top, he was glad to see his feathered companions still asleep with their heads under their wings.

He ate his breakfast, and waited until the birds should start, but they did not leave the place all day. They hopped about from one tree to another looking for food, all day long until the evening, when they went back to their old perch to sleep.

The next day the same thing happened, but on the third morning one bird said to the other, 'Today we must go to the spring to see the Witch-maiden wash her face.' They remained on the tree till noon; then they flew away and went towards the south. The young man's heart beat with anxiety lest he should lose sight of his guides, but he managed to keep the birds in view until they again perched upon a tree. The young man ran after them until he was quite exhausted and out of breath, and after three short rests the birds at length reached a small open space in the forest, on the edge of which they placed themselves on the top of a high tree. When the youth had overtaken them, he saw that there was a clear spring in the middle of the space. He sat down at the foot of the tree upon which the birds were perched, and listened attentively to what they were saying to each other.

'The sun is not down yet,' said the first bird; 'we must wait yet awhile till the moon rises and the maiden comes to the spring. Do you think she will see that young man sitting under the tree?'

'Nothing is likely to escape her eyes, certainly not a young man,' said the other bird. 'Will he have the sense not to let himself be caught in her toils?'

'We will wait,' said the first bird, 'and see how they get on together.'

The evening light had quite faded, and the full moon was already shining down upon the forest, when the young man heard a slight rustling sound. After a few moments there came out of the forest the Witch-maiden, gliding over the grass so lightly that her feet seemed scarcely to touch the ground, and stood beside the spring. The youth could not turn away his eyes from her, for he had never in his life seen a woman so beautiful. Without seeming to notice anything, she went to the spring, looked up to the full moon, then knelt down and bathed her face nine times, then looked up to the moon again and walked nine times round the well, and as she walked she sang this song:

> 'Full-faced moon with light unshaded,
> Let my beauty ne'er be faded.
> Never let my cheek grow pale!
> While the moon is waning nightly,
> May the maiden bloom more brightly,
> May her freshness never fail!'

Then she dried her face with her long hair, and was about to go away, when her eye suddenly fell upon the spot where the young man was sitting, and she turned towards the tree. The youth rose and stood waiting. Then she said, 'You ought to have a heavy punishment because you have presumed to watch my secret doings in the moonlight. But I will forgive you this time, because you are a stranger and knew no better. But you must tell me truly who you are and how you came to this place, where no mortal has ever set foot before.'

The youth answered humbly: 'Forgive me, beautiful maiden, if I have unintentionally offended you. I chanced to come here after long wandering, and found a good place to sleep under this tree. At your coming I did not know what to do, but stayed where I was, because I thought my silent watching could not offend you.'

The Witch-maiden answered kindly, 'Come and spend this night with us. You will sleep better on a pillow than on damp moss.' The youth hesitated for a little, but presently he heard the birds saying from the top of the tree, 'Go where she calls you, but take care to give no blood, or you will sell your soul.'

So the youth went with her, and soon they reached a beautiful garden, where stood a splendid house, which glittered in the moonlight as if it was all built out of gold and silver. When the youth entered he found many splendid chambers, each one finer than the last. Hundreds of tapers burnt upon golden candlesticks, and shed a light like the brightest day. At length they reached a chamber where a table was spread with the most costly dishes. At the table were placed two chairs, one of silver, the other of gold. The Witch-maiden seated herself upon the golden chair, and offered the silver one to her companion. They were served by maidens dressed in white, whose feet made no sound as they moved about, and not a word was spoken during the meal.

Afterwards the youth and the Witch-maiden conversed pleasantly together, until a woman, dressed in red, came in to remind them that it was bedtime. The youth was now shown into another room, containing a silken bed with down cushions, where he slept delightfully, yet he seemed to hear a voice near his bed which repeated to him, 'Remember to give no blood!'

The next morning the Witch-maiden asked him whether he would not like to stay with her always in this beautiful place, and as he did not answer immediately, she continued: 'You see how I always remain young and beautiful, and I am under no one's orders, but can do just what I like, so that I have never thought of marrying before. But from the moment I saw you I took a fancy to you, so if you agree, we might be married and might live together like princes, because I have great riches.'

The youth could not but be tempted with the beautiful maiden's offer, but he remembered how the birds had called her the witch, and their warning always sounded in his ears. Therefore he answered cautiously, 'Do not be angry, dear maiden, if I do not decide immediately on this important matter. Give me a few days to consider before we come to an understanding.'

'Why not?' answered she. 'Take some weeks to consider if you like, and take counsel with your own heart.' And to make the time pass pleasantly, she took the youth over every part of her beautiful dwelling, and showed him all her splendid treasures. But these treasures were all produced by enchantment, for the Witch-maiden could make anything she wished appear by the help of King Solomon's signet ring; only none of these things remained fixed; they passed away like the wind without leaving a trace behind. But the youth did not know this; he thought they were all real.

One day the Witch-maiden took him into a secret chamber, where a little gold box was standing on a silver table. Pointing to the box, she said, 'Here is my greatest treasure, whose like is not to be found in the whole world. It is a precious gold ring. When you marry me, I will give you this ring as a marriage gift, and it will make you the happiest of mortal men. But in order that our love may last for ever, you must give me for the ring three drops of blood from the little finger of your left hand.'

When the youth heard these words, a cold shudder ran over him, for he remembered that his soul was at stake. He was cunning enough, however, to conceal his feelings and to make no direct answer, but he only asked the maiden, as if carelessly, what was remarkable about the ring?

She answered, 'No mortal is able entirely to understand the power of this ring, because no one thoroughly understands the secret signs engraved upon it. But even with my half-knowledge I can work great wonders. If I put the ring upon the little finger of my left hand, then I can fly like a bird through the air wherever I wish to go. If I put it on the third finger of my left hand I am invisible, and I can see everything that passes around me, though no one can see me. If I put the ring upon the middle finger of my left hand, then neither fire nor water nor any sharp weapon can hurt me. If I put it on the forefinger of my left hand, then I can with its help produce whatever I wish. I can in a single moment build houses or anything I desire. Finally, as long as I wear the ring on the thumb of my left hand, that hand is so strong that it can break down rocks and walls. Besides these, the ring has other secret signs which, as I said, no one can understand.

No doubt it contains secrets of great importance. The ring formerly belonged to King Solomon, the wisest of kings, during whose reign the wisest men lived. But it is not known whether this ring was ever made by mortal hands: it is supposed that an angel gave it to the wise King.'

When the youth heard all this, he was determined to try and get possession of the ring, though he did not quite believe in all its wonderful gifts. He wished that the Witch-maiden would let him have it in his hand, but he did not quite like to ask her to do so, and after a while she put it back into the box. A few days after they were again speaking of the magic ring, and the youth said, 'I do not think it possible that the ring can have all the power you say it has.'

Then the Witch-maiden opened the box and took the ring out, and it glittered as she held it like the clearest sunbeam. She put it on the middle finger of her left hand, and told

The Dragon of the North

the youth to take a knife and try as hard as he could to cut her with it, for he would not be able to hurt her. He was unwilling at first, but she insisted. Then he tried, at first only in play, and then seriously, to strike her with the knife, but an invisible wall of iron seemed to be between them, and she stood before him laughing and unhurt. Then she put the ring on her third finger, and in an instant she had vanished from his eyes. Presently she was beside him again laughing, and holding the ring between her fingers.

'Do let me try,' said the youth, 'whether I can do these wonderful things.'

The Witch-maiden, suspecting no treachery, gave him the magic ring.

The youth pretended to have forgotten what to do, and asked what finger he must put the ring on so that no sharp weapon could hurt him?

'Oh, the middle finger of your left hand,' she answered, laughing.

She took the knife and tried to strike the youth, and he even tried to cut himself with it, but found it impossible. Then he asked her to show him how to split stones and rocks with the help of the ring. So she led him into a courtyard where stood a great boulder-stone. 'Now,' she said, 'put the ring upon the thumb of your left hand, and you will see how strong that hand has become. The youth did so, and found to his astonishment that with a single blow of his fist the stone flew into a thousand pieces.

Then the youth bethought him that he who does not use his luck when he has it is a fool, and that this was a chance which once lost might never return. So while they stood laughing at the shattered stone he placed the ring, as if in play, upon the third finger of his left hand.

'Now,' said she, 'you are invisible to me until you take the ring off again.'

But the youth had no mind to do that; on the contrary, he went farther off, then put the ring on the little finger of his left hand, and soared into the air like a bird.

When the Witch-maiden saw him flying away she thought at first that he was still in play, and cried, 'Come back, friend, for now you see I have told you the truth.' But the young man never came back.

Then the Witch-maiden saw she was deceived, and bitterly repented that she had ever trusted him with the ring.

The youth never halted in his flight until he reached the dwelling of the wise magician who had taught him the speech of birds. The magician was delighted to find that his search had been successful, and at once set to work to interpret the secret signs engraved upon the ring, but it took him seven weeks to make them out clearly.

Then he gave the youth the following instructions how to overcome the Dragon of the North: 'You must have an iron horse cast, which must have little wheels under each foot. You must also be armed with a spear two fathoms long, which you will be able to wield by means of the magic ring upon your left thumb. The spear must be as thick in the middle as a large tree, and both its ends must be sharp. In the middle of the spear you must have two strong chains ten fathoms in length. As soon as the Dragon has made himself fast to the spear, which you must thrust through his jaws, you must spring quickly from the iron horse and fasten the ends of the chains firmly to the ground with iron stakes, so that he cannot get away from them. After two or three days the monster's strength will be so far exhausted that you will be able to come near him. Then you can put Solomon's ring upon your left thumb and give him the finishing stroke, but keep the ring on your third finger until you have come close to him, so that the monster cannot see you, else he might strike you dead with his long tail. But when all is done, take care you do not lose the ring, and that no one takes it from you by cunning.'

The young man thanked the magician for his directions, and promised, should they succeed, to reward him. But the magician answered, 'I have profited so much by the wisdom the ring has taught me that I desire no other reward.' Then they parted, and the youth quickly flew home through the air.

After remaining in his own home for some weeks, he heard people say that the terrible Dragon of the North was not far off, and might shortly be expected in the country. The King announced publicly that he would give his daughter in marriage, as well as a large part of his kingdom, to whosoever should free the country from the monster.

The youth then went to the King and told him that he had good hopes of subduing the Dragon, if the King would grant him all he desired for the purpose. The King willingly agreed, and the iron horse, the great spear, and the chains were all prepared as the youth requested. When all was ready, it was found that the iron horse was so heavy that a hundred men could not move it from the spot, so the youth found there was nothing for it but to move it with his own strength by means of the magic ring.

The Dragon was now so near that in a couple of springs he would be over the frontier. The youth now began to consider how he should act, for if he had to push the iron horse from behind he could not ride upon it as the sorcerer had said he must. But a raven unexpectedly gave him this advice: 'Ride upon the horse, and push the spear against the ground, as if you were pushing off a boat from the land.' The youth did so, and found that in this way he could easily move forwards.

The Dragon had his monstrous jaws wide open, all ready for his expected prey. A few paces nearer, and man and horse would have been swallowed up by them! The youth trembled with horror, and his blood ran cold, yet he did not lose his courage; but, holding the iron spear upright in his hand, he brought it down with all his might right through the monster's lower jaw. Then quick as lightning he sprang from his horse before the Dragon had time to shut his mouth. A fearful clap like thunder, which could be heard for miles around, now warned him that the Dragon's jaws had closed upon the spear.

When the youth turned round, he saw the point of the spear sticking up high above the Dragon's upper jaw, and knew that the other end must be fastened firmly to the ground; but the Dragon had got his teeth fixed in the iron horse, which was now useless. The youth now hastened to fasten down the chains to the ground by means of the enormous iron pegs which he had provided.

The death struggle of the monster lasted three days and three nights; in his writhing he beat his tail so violently against the ground, that at ten miles' distance the earth trembled as if with an earthquake. When he at length lost power to move his tail, the youth with the help of the ring took up a stone which twenty ordinary men could not have moved, and beat the Dragon so hard about the head with it that very soon the monster lay lifeless before him.

You can fancy how great was the rejoicing when the news was spread abroad that the terrible monster was dead. His conqueror was received into the city with as much pomp as if he had been the mightiest of kings. The old King did not need to urge his daughter to marry the slayer of the Dragon; he found her already willing to bestow her hand upon this hero, who had done all alone what whole armies had tried in vain to do.

In a few days a magnificent wedding was celebrated, at which the rejoicings lasted four whole weeks, for all the neighbouring kings had met together to thank the man who had freed the world from their common enemy. But everyone forgot amid the general joy that they ought to have buried the Dragon's monstrous body, for it began now to have such a bad smell that no one could live in the neighbourhood, and before long the whole air was poisoned, and a pestilence broke out which destroyed many hundreds of people.

In this distress, the King's son-in-law resolved to seek help once more from the Eastern magician, to whom he at once travelled through the air like a bird by the help of the ring. But there is a proverb which says that ill-gotten gains never prosper, and the Prince found that the stolen ring brought him ill-luck after all.

The Witch-maiden had never rested night nor day until she had found out where the ring was. As soon as she had discovered by means of magical arts that the Prince in the form of a bird was on his way to the Eastern magician, she changed herself into an eagle and watched in the air until the bird she was waiting for came in sight, for she knew him at once by the ring which was hung round his neck by a ribbon. Then the eagle pounced upon the bird, and the moment she seized him in her talons she tore the ring from his neck before the man in bird's shape had time to prevent her. Then the eagle flew down to the earth with her prey, and the two stood face to face once more in human form.

'Now, villain, you are in my power!' cried the Witch-maiden. 'I favoured you with my love, and you repaid me with treachery and theft. You stole my most precious jewel from me, and do you expect to live happily as the King's son-in-law? Now the tables are turned; you are in my power, and I will be revenged on you for your crimes.'

'Forgive me! forgive me!' cried the Prince; 'I know too well how deeply I have wronged you, and most heartily do I repent it.'

The maiden answered, 'Your prayers and your repentance come too late, and if I were to spare you everyone would think me a fool. You have doubly wronged me; first you scorned my love, and then you stole my ring, and you must bear the punishment.'

With these words she put the ring upon her left thumb, lifted the young man with one hand, and walked away with him under her arm. This time she did not take him to a splendid palace, but to a deep cave in a rock, where there were chains hanging from the wall. The Witch-maiden now chained the young man's hands and feet so that he could not escape; then she said in an angry voice, 'Here you shall remain chained up until you die. I will bring you every day enough food to prevent you dying of hunger, but you need never hope for freedom any more.' With these words she left him.

The old King and his daughter waited anxiously for many weeks for the Prince's return, but no news of him arrived. The King's daughter often dreamed that her husband was going through some great suffering; she therefore begged her father to summon all the enchanters and magicians, that they might try to find out where the Prince was and how he could be set free. But the magicians, with all their arts, could find out nothing, except that he was still living and undergoing great suffering; but none could tell where he was to be found.

At last a celebrated magician from Finland was brought before the King, who had found out that the King's son-in-law was imprisoned in the East, not by men, but by some more powerful being. The King now sent messengers to the East to look for his son-in-law, and they by good luck met with the old magician who had interpreted the signs on King Solomon's ring, and thus was possessed of more wisdom than anyone else in the world.

The magician soon found out what he wished to know, and pointed out the place where the Prince was imprisoned, but said: 'He is kept there by enchantment, and cannot be set free without my help. I will therefore go with you myself.'

So they all set out, guided by birds, and after some days came to the cave where the unfortunate Prince had been chained up for nearly seven years. He recognised the magician immediately, but the old man did not know him, he had grown so thin. However, he undid the chains by the help of magic, and took care of the Prince until he recovered and became strong enough to travel. When he reached home he found that the old King had died that morning, so that he was now raised to the throne. And now after his long suffering came prosperity, which lasted to the end of his life; but he never got back the magic ring, nor has it ever again been seen by mortal eyes.

Now, if *you* had been the Prince, would you not rather have stayed with the pretty Witch-maiden?

The Dragon and His Grandmother

There was once a great war, and the King had a great many soldiers, but he gave them so little pay that they could not live upon it. Then three of them took counsel together and determined to desert.

One of them said to the others, 'If we are caught, we shall be hanged on the gallows; how shall we set about it?' The other said, 'Do you see that large cornfield there? If we were to hide ourselves in that, no one could find us. The army cannot come into it, and tomorrow it is to march on.'

They crept into the corn, but the army did not march on, but remained encamped close around them. They sat for two days and two nights in the corn, and grew so hungry that they nearly died; but if they were to venture out, it was certain death.

The Dragon and His Grandmother

They said at last, 'What use was it our deserting? We must perish here miserably.'

Whilst they were speaking, a fiery dragon came flying through the air. It hovered near them, and asked why they were hiding there. They answered, 'We are three soldiers, and have deserted because our pay was so small. Now if we remain here we shall die of hunger, and if we move out we shall be strung up on the gallows.' 'If you will serve me for seven years,' said the Dragon, 'I will lead you through the midst of the army so that no one shall catch you.' 'We have no choice, and must take your offer,' said they. Then the dragon seized them in his claws, took them through the air over the army, and set them down on the earth a long way from it.

He gave them a little whip, saying, 'Whip and slash with this, and as much money as you want will jump up before you. You can then live as great lords, keep horses, and drive about in carriages. But after seven years you are mine.' Then he put a book before them, which he made all three of them sign. 'I will then give you a riddle,' he said, 'if you guess it, you shall be free and out of my power.'

The Dragon then flew away, and they journeyed on with their little whip. They had as much money as they wanted, wore grand clothes, and made their way into the world. Wherever they went they lived in merrymaking and splendour, drove about with horses and carriages, ate and drank, but did nothing wrong.

The time passed quickly away, and when the seven years were nearly ended two of them grew terribly anxious and frightened, but the third made light of it, saying, 'Don't be afraid, brothers, I wasn't born yesterday; I will guess the riddle.' They went into a field, sat down, and the two pulled long faces. An old woman passed by, and asked them why they were so sad. 'Alas! what have you to do with it? You cannot help us.'

'Who knows?' she answered. 'Only confide your trouble in me.' Then they told her that they had become the servants of the Dragon for seven long years, and how he had given them money as plentifully as blackberries; but as they had signed their names they were his, unless when the seven years had passed they could guess a riddle. The old woman said, 'If you would help yourselves, one of you must go into the wood, and there he will come upon a tumble-down building of rocks which looks like a little house. He must go in, and there he will find help.' The two melancholy ones thought, 'That won't save us!' and they remained where they were. But the third and merry one jumped up and went into the wood till he found the rock hut. In the hut sat a very old woman, who was the Dragon's grandmother. She asked him how he came, and what was his business there. He told her all that had happened, and because she was pleased with him she took compassion on him, and said she would help him.

She lifted up a large stone which lay over the cellar, saying, 'Hide yourself there; you can hear all that is spoken in this room. Only sit still and don't stir. When the dragon comes, I will ask him what the riddle is, for he tells me everything; then listen carefully what he answers.'

At midnight the Dragon flew in, and asked for his supper. His grandmother laid the table, and brought out food and drink till he was satisfied, and they ate and drank together. Then in the course of the conversation she asked him what he had done in the day, and how many souls he had conquered.

'I haven't had much luck today,' he said, 'but I have a tight hold on three soldiers.'

'Indeed! Three soldiers!' said she. 'Who cannot escape you?'

'They are mine,' answered the Dragon scornfully, 'for I shall only give them one riddle which they will never be able to guess.'

'What sort of a riddle is it?' she asked.

'I will tell you this. In the North Sea lies a dead sea-cat—that shall be their roast meat; and the rib of a whale—that shall be their silver spoon; and the hollow foot of a dead horse—that shall be their wineglass.'

When the Dragon had gone to bed, his old grandmother pulled up the stone and let out the soldier.

'Did you pay attention to everything?'

'Yes,' he replied, 'I know enough, and can help myself splendidly.'

Then he went by another way through the window secretly, and in all haste back to his comrades. He told them how the Dragon had been outwitted by his grandmother, and how he had heard from his own lips the answer to the riddle.

Then they were all delighted and in high spirits, took out their whip, and cracked so much money that it came jumping up from the ground.

When the seven years had quite gone, the Fiend came with his book, and, pointing at the signatures, said, 'I will take you underground with me; you shall have a meal there. If you can tell me what you will get for your roast meat, you shall be free, and shall also keep the whip.'

Then said the first soldier, 'In the North Sea lies a dead sea-cat; that shall be our roast meat.'

The Dragon was much annoyed, and hummed and hawed a good deal, and asked the second, 'But what shall be your spoon?'

'The rib of a whale shall be our silver spoon.'

The Dragon made a face, and growled again three times, 'Hum, hum, hum,' and said to the third, 'Do you know what your wineglass shall be?'

'An old horse's hoof shall be our wineglass.'

Then the Dragon flew away with a loud shriek, and had no more power over them. But the three soldiers took the little whip, whipped as much money as they wanted, and lived happily to their lives' end.

The Prince and the Dragon

Once upon a time there lived an emperor who had three sons. They were all fine young men, and fond of hunting, and scarcely a day passed without one or other of them going out to look for game.

One morning the eldest of the three princes mounted his horse and set out for a neighbouring forest, where wild animals of all sorts were to be found. He had not long left the castle, when a hare sprang out of a thicket and dashed across the road in front. The young man gave chase at once, and pursued it over hill and dale, till at last the hare took refuge in a mill which was standing by the side of a river. The prince followed and entered the mill, but stopped in terror by the door, for, instead of a hare, before him stood a dragon, breathing fire and flame. At this fearful sight the prince turned to fly, but a fiery tongue coiled round his waist, and drew him into the dragon's mouth, and he was seen no more.

A week passed away, and when the prince never came back everyone in the town began to grow uneasy. At last his next brother told the emperor that he likewise would go out to hunt, and that perhaps he would find some clue as to his brother's disappearance. But hardly had the castle gates closed on the prince than the hare sprang out of the bushes as before, and led the huntsman up hill and down dale, till they reached the mill. Into this the hare flew with the prince at his heels, when, lo! instead of the hare, there stood a dragon breathing fire and flame; and out shot a fiery tongue which coiled round the prince's waist, and lifted him straight into the dragon's mouth, and he was seen no more.

Days went by, and the emperor waited and waited for the sons who never came, and could not sleep at night for wondering where they were and what had become of them. His youngest son wished to go in search of his brothers, but for long the emperor refused to listen to him, lest he should lose him also. But the prince prayed so hard for leave to make the search, and promised so often that he would be very cautious and careful, that at length the emperor gave him permission, and ordered the best horse in the stables to be saddled for him.

Full of hope the young prince started on his way, but no sooner did he go outside the city walls than a hare sprang out of the bushes and ran before him, till they reached the mill. As before, the animal dashed in through the open door, but this time he was not followed by the prince. Wiser than his brothers, the young man turned away, saying to himself: 'There are as good hares in the forest as any that have come out of it, and when I have caught them, I can come back and look for you.' For many hours he rode up and down the mountain, but saw nothing, and at last, tired of waiting, he went back to the mill. Here he found an old woman sitting, whom he greeted pleasantly.

'Good morning to you, little mother,' he said; and the old woman answered: 'Good morning, my son.'

'Tell me, little mother,' went on the prince, 'where shall I find my hare?'

'My son,' replied the old woman, 'that was no hare, but a dragon who has led many men hither, and then has eaten them all.' At these words the prince's heart grew heavy, and he cried, 'Then my brothers must have come here, and have been eaten by the dragon!'

'You have guessed right,' answered the old woman; 'and I can give you no better counsel than to go home at once, before the same fate overtakes you.'

'Will you not come with me out of this dreadful place?' said the young man.

'He took me prisoner, too,' answered she, 'and I cannot shake off his chains.'

'Then listen to me,' cried the prince. 'When the dragon comes back, ask him where he always goes when he leaves here, and what makes him so strong; and when you have coaxed the secret from him, tell me the next time I come.'

So the prince went home, and the old woman remained in the mill, and as soon as the dragon returned she said to him:

'Where have you been all this time—you must have travelled far?'

'Yes, little mother, I have indeed travelled far,' answered he. Then the old woman began to flatter him, and to praise his cleverness; and when she thought she had got him into a good temper, she said: 'I have wondered so often where you get your strength from; I do wish you would tell me. I would stoop and kiss the place out of pure love!' The dragon laughed at this, and answered:

'In the hearthstone yonder lies the secret of my strength.' Then the old woman jumped up and kissed the hearth; whereat the dragon laughed the more, and said:

'You foolish creature! I was only jesting. It is not in the hearthstone, but in that tall tree lies the secret of my strength.' Then the old woman jumped up again and put her arms round the tree, and kissed it heartily. Loudly laughed the dragon when he saw what she was doing.

'Old fool,' he cried, as soon as he could speak, 'did you really believe that my strength came from that tree?'

'Where is it then?' asked the old woman, rather crossly, for she did not like being made fun of.

'My strength,' replied the dragon, 'lies far away; so far that you could never reach it. Far, far from here is a kingdom, and by its capital city is a lake, and in the lake is a dragon, and inside the dragon is a wild boar, and inside the wild boar is a pigeon, and inside the pigeon a sparrow, and inside the sparrow is my strength.' And when the old woman heard this, she thought it was no use flattering him any longer, for never, never, could she take his strength from him.

The following morning, when the dragon had left the mill, the prince came back, and the old woman told him all that the creature had said. He listened in silence, and then returned to the castle, where he put on a suit of shepherd's clothes, and taking a staff in his hand, he went forth to seek a place as tender of sheep.

For some time he wandered from village to village and from town to town, till he came at length to a large city in a distant kingdom, surrounded on three sides by a great lake, which happened to be the very lake in which the dragon lived. As was his custom, he stopped everybody whom he met in the streets that looked likely to want a shepherd and begged them to engage him, but they all seemed to have shepherds of their own, or else not to need any. The prince was beginning to lose heart, when a man who had overheard his question turned round and said that he had better go and ask the emperor, as he was in search of some one to see after his flocks.

'Will you take care of my sheep?' said the emperor, when the young man knelt before him.

'Most willingly, your Majesty,' he answered and listened obediently while the emperor told him what he was to do.

'Outside the city walls,' went on the emperor, 'you will find a large lake, and by its banks lie the richest meadows in my kingdom. When you are leading out your flocks to pasture, they will all run straight to these meadows, and none that have gone there have ever been known to come back. Take heed, therefore, my son, not to suffer your sheep to go where they will, but drive them to any spot that you think best.'

With a low bow the prince thanked the emperor for his warning, and promised to do his best to keep the sheep safe. Then he left the palace and went to the market-place, where he bought two greyhounds, a hawk, and a set of pipes; after that he took the sheep out to pasture. The instant the animals caught sight of the lake lying before them, they trotted off as fast as their legs would go to the green meadows lying round it.

The prince did not try to stop them; he only placed his hawk on the branch of a tree, laid his pipes on the grass, and bade the greyhounds sit still; then, rolling up his sleeves and trousers, he waded into the water crying as he did so: 'Dragon! Dragon! if you are not a coward, come out and fight with me!' And a voice answered from the depths of the lake:

'I am waiting for you, O prince,' and the next minute the dragon reared himself out of the water, huge and horrible to see. The prince sprang upon him and they grappled with each other and fought together till the sun was high, and it was noonday. Then the dragon gasped:

'O prince, let me dip my burning head once into the

lake, and I will hurl you up to the top of the sky.' But the prince answered, 'Oh, ho! My good dragon, do not crow too soon! If the emperor's daughter were only here, and would kiss me on the forehead, I would throw you up higher still!' And suddenly the dragon's hold loosened, and he fell back into the lake.

As soon as it was evening, the prince washed away all signs of the fight, took his hawk upon his shoulder, and his pipes under his arm, and with his greyhounds in front and his flock following after him, he set out for the city. As they all passed through the streets the people stared in wonder, for never before had any flock returned from the lake.

The next morning he rose early, and led his sheep down the road to the lake. This time, however, the emperor sent two men on horseback to ride behind him, with orders to watch the prince all day long. The horsemen kept the prince and his sheep in sight, without being seen themselves. As soon as they beheld the sheep running towards the meadows, they turned aside up a steep hill, which overhung the lake.

When the shepherd reached the place he laid, as before, his pipes on the grass and bade the greyhounds sit beside them, while the hawk he perched on the branch of the tree. Then he rolled up his trousers and his sleeves, and waded into the water crying:

'Dragon! Dragon! If you are not a coward, come out and fight with me!' And the dragon answered:

'I am waiting for you, O prince,' and the next minute

he reared himself out of the water, huge and horrible to see. Again they clasped each other tight round the body and fought till it was noon, and when the sun was at its hottest, the dragon gasped:

'O prince, let me dip my burning head once in the lake, and I will hurl you up to the top of the sky.' But the prince answered:

'Oh, ho! My good dragon, do not crow too soon! If the emperor's daughter were only here, and would kiss me on the forehead, I would throw you up higher still!' And suddenly the dragon's hold loosened, and he fell back into the lake.

As soon as it was evening, the prince again collected his sheep, and playing on his pipes he marched before them into the city. When he passed through the gates all the people came out of their houses to stare in wonder, for never before had any flock returned from the lake.

Meanwhile, the two horsemen had ridden quickly back, and told the emperor all that they had seen and heard. The emperor listened eagerly to their tale, then called his daughter to him and repeated it to her.

'Tomorrow,' he said, when he had finished, 'you shall go with the shepherd to the lake, and then you shall kiss him on the forehead as he wishes.'

But when the princess heard these words, she burst into tears, and sobbed out:

'Will you really send me, your only child, to that dreadful place, from which most likely I shall never come back?'

'Fear nothing, my little daughter, all will be well. Many shepherds have gone to that lake and none have ever returned; but this one has in these two days fought twice with the dragon and has escaped without a wound. So I hope tomorrow he will kill the dragon altogether, and deliver this land from the monster who has slain so many of our bravest men.'

Scarcely had the sun begun to peep over the hills next morning, when the princess stood by the shepherd's side, ready to go to the lake. The shepherd was brimming over with joy, but the princess only wept bitterly. 'Dry your tears, I implore you,' said he. 'If you will just do what I ask you, and when the time comes, run and kiss my forehead, you have nothing to fear.'

Merrily the shepherd blew on his pipes as he marched at the head of his flock, only stopping every now and then to say to the weeping girl at his side:

'Do not cry so, Heart of Gold; trust me and fear nothing.' And so they reached the lake.

In an instant the sheep were scattered all over the meadows, and the prince placed his hawk on the tree, and his pipes on the grass, while he bade his greyhounds lie beside them. Then he rolled up his trousers and his sleeves, and waded into the water, calling:

'Dragon! Dragon! If you are not a coward, come forth, and let us have one more fight together.' And the dragon answered:

'I am waiting for you, O prince,' and the next minute he reared himself out of the water, huge and horrible to see.

Swiftly he drew near to the bank, and the prince sprang to meet him, and they grasped each other round the body and fought till it was noonday. And when the sun was at its hottest, the dragon cried:

'O prince, let me dip my burning head in the lake, and I will hurl you to the top of the sky.' But the prince answered:

'Oh, ho! My good dragon, do not crow too soon! If the emperor's daughter were only here, and she would kiss my forehead, I would throw you higher still.'

Hardly had he spoken when the princess, who had been listening, ran up and kissed him on the forehead. Then the prince swung the dragon straight up into the clouds, and when he touched the earth again, he broke into a thousand pieces. Out of the pieces there sprang a wild boar and galloped away, but the prince called his hounds to give chase, and they caught the boar and tore it to bits. Out of the pieces there sprang a hare, and in a moment the greyhounds were after it, and they caught it and killed it; and out of the hare there came a pigeon.

Quickly the prince let loose his hawk, which soared straight into the air, then swooped upon the bird and brought it to his master. The prince cut open its body and found the sparrow inside, as the old woman had said.

'Now,' cried the prince, holding the sparrow in his hand, 'now you shall tell me where I can find my brothers.'

'Do not hurt me,' answered the sparrow, 'and I will tell you with all my heart.' Behind your father's castle stands a mill, and in the mill are three slender twigs. Cut off these twigs and strike their roots with them, and the iron door of a cellar will open. In the cellar you will find as many people, young and old, women and children, as would fill a kingdom, and among them are your brothers.'

By this time twilight had fallen, so the prince washed himself in the lake, took the hawk on his shoulder and the pipes under his arm, and with his greyhounds before him and his flock behind him, marched gaily into the town, the princess following them all, still trembling with fright. And so they passed through the streets, thronged with a wondering crowd, till they reached the castle.

Unknown to anyone, the emperor had stolen out on horseback, and had hidden himself on the hill, where he could see all that happened. When all was over, and the power of the dragon was broken for ever, he rode quickly back to the castle, and was ready to receive the prince with open arms, and to promise him his daughter to wife.

The wedding took place with great splendour, and for a whole week the town was hung with coloured lamps, and tables were spread in the hall of the castle for all who chose to come and eat.

And when the feast was over, the prince told the emperor and the people who he really was, and at this everyone rejoiced still more, and preparations were made for the prince and princess to return to their own kingdom, for the prince was impatient to set free his brothers.

The first thing he did when he reached his native country was to hasten to the mill, where he found the three twigs as the sparrow had told him. The moment he struck the root, the iron door flew open, and from the cellar a countless multitude of men and women streamed forth. He bade them go one by one wheresoever they would, while he himself waited by the door till his brothers passed through. How delighted they were to meet again, and to hear all that the prince had done to deliver them from their enchantment. And they went home with him and served him all the days of their lives, for they said that he only who had proved himself brave and faithful was fit to be king.

Beauty and the Beast

Once upon a time, in a very far-off country, there lived a merchant who had been so fortunate in all his undertakings that he was enormously rich. As he had, however, six sons and six daughters, he found that his money was not too much to let them all have everything they fancied, as they were accustomed to do.

But one day a most unexpected misfortune befell them. Their house caught fire and was speedily burnt to the ground, with all the splendid furniture, the books, pictures, gold, silver and precious goods it contained; and this was only the beginning of their troubles. Their father, who had until this moment prospered in all ways, suddenly lost every ship he had upon the sea, either by dint of pirates, shipwreck or fire. Then he heard that his clerks in distant countries, whom he trusted entirely, had proved unfaithful; and at last from great wealth he fell into the direst poverty.

All that he had left was a little house in a desolate place at least a hundred leagues from the town in which he had lived, and to this he was forced to retreat with his children, who were in despair at the idea of leading such a different life. Indeed, the daughters at first hoped that their friends, who had been so numerous while they were rich, would insist on their staying in their houses now that they no longer possessed one. But they soon found that they were left alone, and that their former friends even attributed their misfortunes to their extravagance, and showed no intention of offering them any help.

So nothing was left for them but to take their departure to the cottage, which stood in the midst of a dark forest, and seemed to be the most dismal place upon the face of the earth. As they were too poor to have any servants, the girls had to work hard, like peasants, and the sons, for their part, cultivated the fields to earn their living. Roughly clothed, and living in the simplest way, the girls regretted unceasingly the luxuries and amusements of their former life; only the youngest tried to be brave and cheerful.

She had been as sad as anyone when misfortune overtook her father, but, soon recovering her natural gaiety, she set to work to make the best of things, to amuse her father and brothers as well as she could, and to try to persuade her sisters to join her in dancing and singing. But they would do nothing of the sort, and, because she was not as doleful as themselves, they declared that this miserable life was all she was fit for. But she was really far prettier and cleverer than they were; indeed, she was so lovely that she was always called Beauty.

After two years, when they were all beginning to get used to their new life, something happened to disturb their tranquillity. Their father received the news that one of his ships, which he had believed to be lost, had come safely into port with a rich cargo. All the sons and daughters at once thought that their poverty was at an end, and wanted to set out directly for the town; but their father, who was more prudent, begged them to wait a little, and, though it was harvest time, and he could ill be spared, determined to go himself first, to make inquiries.

Only the youngest daughter had any doubt but that they would soon again be as rich as they were before, or at least rich enough to live comfortably in some town where they would find amusement and gay companions once more. So they all loaded their father with commissions for jewels and dresses which it would have taken a fortune to buy; only Beauty, feeling sure that it was of no use, did not ask for anything. Her father, noticing her silence, said: 'And what shall I bring for you, Beauty?'

'The only thing I wish for is to see you come home safely,' she answered.

But this only vexed her sisters, who fancied she was blaming them for having asked for such costly things. Her father, however, was pleased, but as he thought that at her age she certainly ought to like pretty presents, he told her to choose something.

'Well, dear father,' she said, 'as you insist upon it, I beg that you will bring me a rose. I have not seen one since we came here, and I love them so much.'

So the merchant set out and reached the town as quickly as possible, but only to find that his former companions, believing him to be dead, had divided among them the goods which the ship had brought; and after six months of trouble and expense he found himself as poor as when he started, having been able to recover only just enough to pay the cost of his journey.

To make matters worse, he was obliged to leave the town in the most terrible weather, so that by the time he was within a few leagues of his home he was almost exhausted with cold and fatigue. Though he knew it would take some hours to get through the forest, he was so anxious to be at his journey's end that he resolved to go on; but night overtook him, and the deep snow and bitter frost made it impossible for his horse to carry him any further. Not a house was to be seen; the only shelter he could get was the hollow trunk of a great tree, and there he crouched all night which seemed to him the longest he had ever known. In spite of his weariness, the howling of the wolves kept him awake, and even when at last the day broke, he was not much better off, for the falling snow had covered up every path, and he did not know which way to turn.

At length he made out some sort of track, and though at the beginning it was so rough and slippery that he fell down more than once, it presently became easier, and led him into an avenue of trees which ended in a splendid castle. It seemed to the merchant very strange that no snow had fallen in the avenue, which was entirely composed of orange trees, covered with flowers and fruit.

When he reached the first court of the castle he saw before him a flight of agate steps, and went up them, and passed through several splendidly furnished rooms. The pleasant warmth of the air revived him, and he felt very hungry; but there seemed to be nobody in all this vast and splendid palace whom he could ask to give him something to eat.

Deep silence reigned everywhere, and at last, tired of roaming through empty rooms and galleries, he stopped in a room smaller than the rest, where a clear fire was burning and a couch was drawn up closely to it. Thinking that this must be prepared for someone who was expected, he sat down to wait till he should come, and very soon fell into a sweet sleep.

When his extreme hunger wakened him after several hours, he was still alone; but a little table, upon which was a good dinner, had been drawn up close to him, and, as he had eaten nothing for twenty-four hours, he lost no time in beginning his meal, hoping that he might soon have an opportunity of thanking his considerate entertainer, whoever it might be.

But no one appeared, and even after another long sleep, from which he awoke completely refreshed, there was no sign of anybody, though a fresh meal of dainty cakes and fruit was prepared upon the little table at his elbow. Being naturally timid, the silence began to terrify him, and he resolved to search once more through all the rooms; but it was of no use. Not even a servant was to be seen; there was no sign of life in the palace!

He began to wonder what he should do, and to amuse himself by pretending that all the treasures he saw were his own, and considering how he would divide them among his children. Then he went down into the garden, and though it was winter everywhere else, here the sun shone, and the birds sang, and the flowers bloomed, and the air was soft and sweet. The merchant, in ecstasies with all he saw and heard, said to himself:

'All this must be meant for me. I will go this minute and bring my children to share all these delights.'

In spite of being so cold and weary when he reached the castle, he had taken his horse to the stable and fed it. Now he thought he would saddle it for his homeward journey, and he turned down the path which led to the stable. This path had a hedge of roses on each side of it, and the merchant thought he had never seen or smelt such exquisite flowers. They reminded him of his promise to Beauty, and he stopped and had just gathered one to take to her when he was startled by a strange noise behind him. Turning round, he saw a frightful Beast, which seemed to be very angry and said, in a terrible voice:

'Who told you that you might gather my roses? Was it not enough that I allowed you to be in my palace and was kind to you? This is the way you show your gratitude, by stealing my flowers! But your insolence shall not go unpunished.' The merchant, terrified by these furious words, dropped the fatal rose, and, throwing himself on his knees, cried: 'Pardon me, noble sir. I am truly grateful to you for your hospitality, which was so magnificent that I could not imagine that you would be offended by my taking such a little thing as a rose.' But the Beast's anger was not lessened by this speech.

'You are already prepared with excuses and flattery,' he cried, 'but that will not save you from the death you deserve.'

'Alas!' thought the merchant, 'If my daughter could only know what danger her rose has brought me into!'

And in despair he began to tell the Beast all his misfortunes, and the reason of his journey, not forgetting to mention Beauty's request.

'A king's ransom would hardly have procured all that my other daughters asked,' he said: 'but I thought that I might at least take Beauty her rose. I beg you to forgive me, for you see I meant no harm.'

The Beast considered for a moment, and then he said, in a less furious tone:

'I will forgive you on one condition—you have to give me one of your daughters.'

'Ah!' cried the merchant, 'if I were cruel enough to buy my own life at the expense of one of my children's, what excuse could I invent to bring her here?'

'No excuse would be necessary,' answered the Beast. 'If she comes at all she must come willingly. On no other condition shall I have her. See if any one of them is courageous enough, and loves you well enough to come and save your life. You seem to be an honest man, so I will trust you to go home. I give you a month to see if either of your daughters will come back with you and stay here, to let you go free. If neither of them is willing, you must come alone, after bidding them goodbye for ever, for then you will belong to me. And do not imagine that you can hide from me, for if you fail to keep your word

I will come and fetch you!' added the Beast grimly.

The merchant accepted this proposal, though he did not really think any of his daughters could be persuaded to come. He promised to return at the time appointed, and then, anxious to escape from the presence of the Beast, he asked permission to set off at once. But the Beast answered that he could not go until next day.

'Then you will find a horse ready for you,' he said. 'Now go and eat your supper, and await my orders.'

The poor merchant, more dead than alive, went back to his room, where the most delicious supper was already served on the little table which was drawn up before a blazing fire. But he was too terrified to eat, and only tasted a few of the dishes, fearing the Beast should be angry if he did not obey his orders.

When he had finished he heard a great noise in the next room, which he knew meant that the Beast was coming. As he could do nothing to escape his visit, the only thing that remained was to seem as little afraid as possible; so when the Beast appeared and asked roughly if he had supped well, the merchant answered humbly that he had. Then the Beast warned him to remember their agreement, and to prepare his daughter exactly for what she had to expect.

'Do not get up tomorrow,' he added, 'until you see the sun and hear a golden bell ring. Then you will find your breakfast waiting for you here, and the horse you are to ride will be ready in the courtyard. He will also bring you back again when you come with your daughter a month hence. Farewell. Take a rose to Beauty, and remember your promise!'

The merchant was only too glad when the Beast went away, and though he could not sleep for sadness, he lay down until the sun rose. Then, after a hasty breakfast, he went to gather Beauty's rose, and mounted his horse, which carried him off so swiftly that in an instant he had lost sight of the palace, and he was still wrapped in gloomy thoughts when it stopped before the door of the cottage.

His sons and daughters, who had been very uneasy at his long absence, rushed to meet him, eager to know the result of his journey, which, seeing him mounted upon a splendid horse and wrapped in a rich mantle, they supposed to be favorable. He hid the truth from them at first, only saying sadly to Beauty as he gave her the rose:

'Here is what you asked me to bring you; you little know what it has cost.'

But this excited their curiosity so greatly that presently he told them his adventures from beginning to end, and then they were all very unhappy. The girls lamented loudly over their lost hopes, and the sons declared that their father should not return to this terrible castle, and began to make plans for killing the Beast if it should come to fetch him.

But he reminded them that he had promised to go back. Then the girls were very angry with Beauty, and said it was all her fault, and that if she had asked for something sensible this would never have happened, and complained bitterly that they should have to suffer for her folly.

Poor Beauty, much distressed, said to them:

'I have, indeed, caused this misfortune, but I assure you I did it innocently. Who could have guessed that to ask for a rose in the middle of summer would cause so much misery? But as I did the mischief, it is just that only I should suffer for it. I will therefore go back with my father to keep his promise.' At first nobody would hear of this arrangement, and her father and brothers, who loved her dearly, declared that nothing should make them let her go; but Beauty was firm.

As the time drew near, she divided all her little possessions between her sisters, and said goodbye to everything she loved, and when the fatal day came she encouraged and cheered her father as they mounted together the horse which had brought him back. It seemed to fly rather than gallop, but so smoothly that Beauty was not frightened; indeed, she would have enjoyed the journey if she had not feared what might happen to her at the end of it. Her father still tried to persuade her to go back, but in vain.

While they were talking the night fell, and then, to their great surprise, wonderful colored lights began to shine in all directions, and splendid fireworks blazed out before them; all the forest was illuminated by them, and even felt pleasantly warm, though it had been bitterly cold before. This lasted until they reached the avenue of orange trees, where were statues holding flaming torches, and when they got nearer to the palace, they saw that it was illuminated from the roof to the ground, and music sounded softly from the courtyard.

'The Beast must be very hungry,' said Beauty, trying to laugh, 'if he makes all this rejoicing over the arrival of his prey.'

But, in spite of her anxiety, she could not help admiring all the wonderful things she saw.

The horse stopped at the foot of the flight of steps leading to the terrace, and when they had dismounted, her father led her to the little room he had been in before, where they found a splendid fire burning, and the table daintily spread with a delicious supper.

The merchant knew that this was meant for them, and Beauty, who was rather less frightened now that she had passed through so many rooms and seen nothing of the Beast, was quite willing to begin, for her long ride had made her very hungry. But they had hardly finished their meal when the noise of the Beast's footsteps was heard approaching, and Beauty clung to her father in terror, which became all the greater when she saw how frightened he was. But when the Beast really appeared, though she trembled at the sight of him, she made a great effort to hide her terror, and saluted him respectfully.

This evidently pleased the Beast. After looking at her he said, in a tone that might have struck terror into the boldest heart, though he did not seem to be angry:

'Good evening, old man. Good evening, Beauty.'

The merchant was too terrified to reply, but Beauty answered sweetly: 'Good evening, Beast.'

'Have you come willingly?' asked the Beast. 'Will you be content to stay here when your father goes away?'

Beauty answered bravely that she was quite prepared to stay. 'I am pleased with you,' said the Beast. 'As you have come of your own accord, you may stay. As for you, old man,' he added, turning to the merchant, 'at sunrise tomorrow you will take your departure. When the bell rings, get up quickly and eat your breakfast, and you will find the same horse waiting to take you home; but remember that you must never expect to see my palace again.'

Then turning to Beauty, he said:

'Take your father into the next room, and help him to choose everything you think your brothers and sisters would like to have. You will find two traveling-trunks there; fill them as full as you can. It is only just that you should send them something precious as a remembrance of yourself.'

Then he went away, after saying, 'Goodbye, Beauty; goodbye, old man,' and though Beauty was beginning to think with great dismay of her father's departure, she was afraid to disobey the Beast's orders; and they went into the next room, which had shelves and cupboards all round it.

They were greatly surprised at the riches it contained. There were splendid dresses fit for a queen, with all the ornaments that were to be worn with them; and when Beauty opened the cupboards she was quite dazzled by the gorgeous jewels that lay in heaps upon every shelf. After choosing a vast quantity, which she divided between her sisters—for she had made a heap of the wonderful dresses for each of them—she opened the last chest, which was full of gold.

'I think, father,' she said, 'that, as the gold will be more useful to you, we had better take out the other things again, and fill the trunks with it.' So they did this; but the more they put in the more room there seemed to be, and at last they put back all the jewels and dresses they had taken out, and Beauty even added as many more of the jewels as she could carry at once; and then the trunks were not too full, but they were so heavy that an elephant could not have carried them!

'The Beast was mocking us,' cried the merchant; 'He must have pretended to give us all these things, knowing that I could not carry them away.'

'Let us wait and see,' answered Beauty. 'I cannot believe that he meant to deceive us. All we can do is to fasten them up and leave them ready.'

So they did this and returned to the little room, where, to their astonishment, they found breakfast ready. The merchant ate his with a good appetite, as the Beast's generosity made him believe that he might perhaps venture to come back soon and see Beauty. But she felt sure that her father was leaving her forever, so she was sad when the bell rang sharply for the second time, and warned them that the time had come for them to part.

They went down into the courtyard, where two horses were waiting, one loaded with the two trunks, the other for him to ride. They were pawing the ground impatiently to start, and the merchant was forced to bid Beauty a hasty farewell; and as soon as he was mounted, he went off at such a pace that she lost sight of him in an instant. Then Beauty began to cry, and wandered sadly back to her own room. But she soon found that she was sleepy, and as she had nothing better to do, she lay down and instantly fell asleep.

And then she dreamed that she was walking by a brook bordered with trees, and lamenting her sad fate, when a young prince, handsomer than anyone she had ever seen, and with a voice that went straight to her heart, came and said to her, 'Ah, Beauty! You are not so unfortunate as you suppose. Here you will be rewarded for all you have suffered elsewhere. Your every wish shall be gratified. Only try to find me out, no matter how I may be disguised, as I love you dearly, and in making me happy you will find your own happiness. Be as true-hearted as you are beautiful, and we shall have nothing left to wish for.' 'What can I do, Prince, to make you happy?' said Beauty. 'Only be grateful,' he answered, 'and do not trust too much to your eyes. And, above all, do not desert me until you have saved me from my cruel misery.'

After this she thought she found herself in a room with a stately and beautiful lady, who said to her:

'Dear Beauty, try not to regret all you have left behind you, for you are destined to a better fate. Only do not let yourself be deceived by appearances.'

Beauty found her dreams so interesting that she was in no hurry to awake, but presently the clock roused her by calling her name softly twelve times, and then she got up and found her dressing-table set out with everything she could possibly want; and when her toilet was finished she found dinner was waiting in the room next to hers. But dinner does not take very long when you are all by yourself, and very soon she sat down cosily in the corner of a sofa, and began to think about the charming Prince she had seen in her dream.

'He said I could make him happy,' said Beauty to herself. 'It seems, then, that this horrible Beast keeps him a prisoner. How can I set him free? I wonder why they both told me not to trust to appearances? I don't understand it. But, after all, it was only a dream, so why should I trouble myself about it? I had better go and find something to do to amuse myself.'

So she got up and began to explore some of the many rooms of the palace.

The first she entered was lined with mirrors, and Beauty saw herself reflected on every side, and thought she had never seen such a charming room. Then a bracelet which was hanging from a chandelier caught her eye, and on taking it down she was greatly surprised to find that it held a portrait of her unknown admirer, just as she had seen him in her dream. With great delight she slipped the bracelet on her arm, and went on into a gallery of pictures, where she soon found a portrait of the same handsome Prince, as large as life, and so well painted that as she studied it he seemed to smile kindly at her. Tearing herself away from the portrait at last, she passed through into a room which contained every musical instrument under the sun, and here she amused herself for a long while in trying some of them, and singing until she was tired.

The next room was a library, and she saw everything she had ever wanted to read, as well as everything she had read, and it seemed to her that a whole lifetime would not be enough to even read the names of the books, there were so many. By this time it was growing dusk, and wax candles in diamond and ruby candlesticks were beginning to light themselves in every room.

Beauty found her supper served just at the time she preferred to have it, but she did not see anyone or hear a sound, and though her father had warned her that she would be alone, she began to find it rather dull.

But presently she heard the Beast coming, and wondered tremblingly if he meant to eat her up now.

However, as he did not seem at all ferocious, and only said gruffly:

'Good evening, Beauty,' she answered cheerfully and managed to conceal her terror. Then the Beast asked her how she had been amusing herself, and she told him all the rooms she had seen.

Then he asked if she thought she could be happy in his palace; and Beauty answered that everything was so beautiful that she would be hard to please if she could not be happy. And after about an hour's talk Beauty began to think that the Beast was not nearly so terrible as she had supposed at first. Then he got up to leave her, and said in his gruff voice:

'Do you love me, Beauty? Will you marry me?'

'Oh! What shall I say?' cried Beauty, for she was afraid to make the Beast angry by refusing.

'Say "yes" or "no" without fear,' he replied.

'Oh! no, Beast,' said Beauty hastily.

'Since you will not, good night, Beauty,' he said.

And she answered, 'Good night, Beast,' very glad to find that her refusal had not provoked him. And after he was gone she was soon in bed and asleep, and dreaming of her unknown Prince. She thought he came and said to her:

'Ah, Beauty! Why are you so unkind to me? I fear I am fated to be unhappy for many a long day still.'

And then her dreams changed, but the charming Prince figured in them all; and when morning came her first thought was to look at the portrait, and see if it was really like him, and she found that it certainly was.

This morning she decided to amuse herself in the garden, for the sun shone, and all the fountains were playing; but she was astonished to find that every place was familiar to her, and presently she came to the brook where the myrtle trees were growing where she had first met the Prince in her dream, and that made her think more than ever that he must be kept a prisoner by the Beast. When she was tired she went back to the palace, and found a new room full of materials for every kind of work—ribbons to make into bows, and silks to work into flowers. Then there was an aviary full of rare birds, which were so tame that they flew to Beauty as soon as they saw her, and perched upon her shoulders and her head.

'Pretty little creatures,' she said, 'how I wish that your cage was nearer to my room, that I might often hear you sing!'

So saying she opened a door, and found, to her delight, that it led into her own room, though she had thought it was quite the other side of the palace.

There were more birds in a room farther on, parrots and cockatoos that could talk, and they greeted Beauty by her name; indeed, she found them so entertaining that she took one or two back to her room, and they talked to her while she was at supper; after which the Beast paid her his usual visit, and asked her the same questions as before, and then with a gruff 'Good night' he took his departure, and Beauty went to bed to dream of her mysterious Prince.

The days passed swiftly in different amusements, and after a while Beauty found out another strange thing in the palace, which often pleased her when she was tired of being alone. There was one room which she had not noticed particularly; it was empty, except that under each of the windows stood a very comfortable chair; and the first time she had looked out of the window it had seemed to her that a black curtain prevented her from seeing anything outside. But the second time she went into the room, happening to be tired, she sat down in one of the chairs, when instantly the curtain was rolled aside, and a most amusing pantomime was acted before her; there were dances, and colored lights, and music, and pretty dresses, and it was all so gay that Beauty was in ecstasies. After that she tried the other seven windows in turn, and there was some new and surprising entertainment to be seen from each of them, so that Beauty never could feel lonely any more.

Every evening after supper the Beast came to see her, and always before saying good night asked her in his terrible voice:

'Beauty, will you marry me?'

And it seemed to Beauty, now she understood him better, that when she said, 'No, Beast,' he went away quite sad. But her happy dreams of the handsome young Prince soon made her forget the poor Beast, and the only thing that at all disturbed her was to be constantly told to distrust appearances, to let her heart guide her, and not her eyes, and many other equally perplexing things, which, consider as she would, she could not understand.

So everything went on for a long time, until at last, happy as she was, Beauty began to long for the sight of her father and her brothers and sisters; and one night, seeing her look very sad, the Beast asked her what was the matter. Beauty had quite ceased to be afraid of him. Now she knew that he was really gentle in spite of his ferocious looks and his dreadful voice. So she answered that she was longing to see her home once more. Upon hearing this the Beast seemed sadly distressed, and cried miserably.

'Ah! Beauty, have you the heart to desert an unhappy Beast like this? What more do you want to make you happy? Is it because you hate me that you want to escape?'

'No, dear Beast,' answered Beauty softly, 'I do not hate you, and I should be very sorry never to see you any more, but I long to see my father again. Only let me go for two months, and I promise to come back to you and stay for the rest of my life.'

The Beast, who had been sighing dolefully while she spoke, now replied:

'I cannot refuse you anything you ask, even though it should cost me my life. Take the four boxes you will find in the room next to your own, and fill them with everything you wish to take with you. But remember your promise and come back when the two months are over, or you may have cause to repent it, for if you do not come in good time you will find your faithful Beast dead. You will not need any chariot to bring you back. Only say goodbye to all your brothers and sisters the night before you come away, and when you have gone to bed turn this ring round upon your finger and say firmly: "I wish to go back to my palace and see my Beast again." Good night, Beauty. Fear nothing, sleep peacefully, and before long you shall see your father once more.'

As soon as Beauty was alone, she hastened to fill the boxes with all the rare and precious things she saw about her, and only when she was tired of heaping things into them did they seem to be full.

Then she went to bed, but could hardly sleep for joy. And when at last she did begin to dream of her beloved Prince she was grieved to see him stretched upon a grassy bank, sad and weary, and hardly like himself.

'What is the matter?' she cried.

He looked at her reproachfully, and said:

'How can you ask me, cruel one? Are you not leaving me to my death perhaps?'

'Ah! Don't be so sorrowful,' cried Beauty; 'I am only going to assure my father that I am safe and happy. I have promised the Beast faithfully that I will come back, and he would die of grief if I did not keep my word!'

'What would that matter to you?' said the Prince 'Surely you would not care?'

'Indeed, I should be ungrateful if I did not care for such a kind Beast,' cried Beauty indignantly. 'I would die to save him from pain. I assure you it is not his fault that he is so ugly.'

Just then a strange sound woke her—someone was speaking not very far away; and opening her eyes she found herself in a room she had never seen before, which was certainly not nearly so splendid as those she was used to in the Beast's palace.

Where could she be? She got up and dressed hastily, and then saw that the boxes she had packed the night before were all in the room. While she was wondering by what magic the Beast had transported them and herself to this strange place, she suddenly heard her father's voice, and rushed out and greeted him joyfully. Her brothers and sisters were all astonished at her appearance, as they had never expected to see her again, and there was no end to the questions they asked her.

She had also much to hear about what had happened to them while she was away, and of her father's journey home. But when they heard that she had only come to be with them for a short time, and then must go back to the Beast's palace for ever, they lamented loudly. Then Beauty asked her father what he thought could be the meaning of her strange dreams, and why the Prince constantly begged her not to trust to appearances.

After much consideration, he answered: 'You tell me

yourself that the Beast, frightful as he is, loves you dearly, and deserves your love and gratitude for his gentleness and kindness; I think the Prince must mean you to understand that you ought to reward him by doing as he wishes you to, in spite of his ugliness.'

Beauty could not help seeing that this seemed very probable; still, when she thought of her dear Prince who was so handsome, she did not feel at all inclined to marry the Beast. At any rate, for two months she need not decide, but could enjoy herself with her sisters. But though they were rich now, and lived in town again, and had plenty of acquaintances, Beauty found that nothing amused her very much; and she often thought of the palace, where she was so happy, especially as at home she never once dreamed of her dear Prince, and she felt quite sad without him.

Then her sisters seemed to have got quite used to being without her, and even found her rather in the way, so she would not have been sorry when the two months were over but for her father and brothers, who begged her to stay, and seemed so grieved at the thought of her departure that she had not the courage to say goodbye to them. Every day when she got up she meant to say it at night, and when night came she put it off again, until at last she had a dismal dream which helped her to make up her mind.

She thought she was wandering in a lonely path in the palace gardens, when she heard groans which seemed to come from some bushes hiding the entrance of a cave, and running quickly to see what could be the matter, she found the Beast stretched out upon his side, apparently dying. He reproached her faintly with being the cause of his distress, and at the same moment a stately lady appeared, and said very gravely:

'Ah! Beauty, you are only just in time to save his life. See what happens when people do not keep their promises! If you had delayed one day more, you would have found him dead.'

Beauty was so terrified by this dream that the next morning she announced her intention of going back at once, and that very night she said goodbye to her father and all her brothers and sisters, and as soon as she was in bed, she turned her ring round upon her finger, and said firmly, 'I wish to go back to my palace and see my Beast again,' as she had been told to do.

Then she fell asleep instantly, and only woke up to hear the clock saying 'Beauty, Beauty' twelve times in its musical voice, which told her at once that she was really in the palace once more. Everything was just as before, and her birds were so glad to see her! But Beauty thought she had never known such a long day, for she was so anxious to see the Beast again that she felt as if suppertime would never come.

But when it did come and no Beast appeared she was really frightened; so, after listening and waiting for a long time, she ran down into the garden to search for him. Up and down the paths and avenues ran poor Beauty, calling him in vain, for no one answered, and not a trace of him could she find; until at last, quite tired, she stopped for a minute's rest, and saw that she was standing opposite the shady path she had seen in her dream. She rushed down it, and, sure enough, there was the cave, and in it lay the Beast—asleep, as Beauty thought. Quite glad to have found him, she ran up and stroked his head, but, to her horror, he did not move or open his eyes.

'Oh! he is dead; and it is all my fault,' said Beauty, crying bitterly.

But then, looking at him again, she fancied he still breathed, and, hastily fetching some water from the nearest fountain, she sprinkled it over his face, and, to her great delight, he began to revive.

'Oh! Beast, how you frightened me!' she cried. 'I never knew how much I loved you until just now, when I feared I was too late to save your life.'

'Can you really love such an ugly creature like me?' said the Beast faintly. 'Ah! Beauty, you only came just in time. I was dying because I thought you had forgotten your promise. But go back now and rest, I shall see you again by and by.'

Beauty, who had half expected that he would be angry with her, was reassured by his gentle voice, and went back to the palace, where supper was awaiting her; and afterward the Beast came in as usual, and talked about the time she had spent with her father, asking if she had enjoyed herself, and if they had all been very glad to see her.

Beauty answered politely, and quite enjoyed telling him all that had happened to her. And when at last the time came for him to go, and he asked, as he had so often asked before,

'Beauty, will you marry me?'

She answered softly, 'Yes, dear Beast.'

As she spoke, a blaze of light sprang up before the windows of the palace; fireworks crackled and guns banged, and across the avenue of orange trees, in letters all made of fireflies, was written: 'Long live the Prince and his Bride.'

Turning to ask the Beast what it could all mean, Beauty found that he had disappeared, and in his place stood her long-loved Prince! At the same moment the wheels of a chariot were heard upon the terrace, and two ladies entered the room. One of them Beauty recognized as the stately lady she had seen in her dreams; the other was also so grand and queenly that Beauty hardly knew which to greet first.

But the one she already knew said to her companion: 'Well, Queen, this is Beauty, who has had the courage to rescue your son from the terrible enchantment. They love one another, and only your consent to their marriage is wanting to make them perfectly happy.'

'I consent with all my heart,' cried the Queen. 'How can I ever thank you enough, charming girl, for having restored my dear son to his natural form?'

And then she tenderly embraced Beauty and the Prince, who had meanwhile been greeting the Fairy and receiving her congratulations.

'Now,' said the Fairy to Beauty, 'I suppose you would like me to send for all your brothers and sisters to dance at your wedding?'

And so she did, and the marriage was celebrated the very next day with the utmost splendor, and Beauty and the Prince lived happily ever after.

The Dragon's Tail

I wonder if the girls and boys who read these stories, have heard of the charming and romantic town of Eisenach? I suppose not, for it is a curious fact that few English people visit the place, though very many Americans go there. Americans are well known to have a special interest in old places with historical associations, because they have nothing of the sort in America; moreover many of them are Germans by birth, and have heard stories of the Wartburg, that beautiful old castle, which from the summit of a hill, surrounded by woods, overlooks the town of Eisenach.

The Wartburg is quaintly built with dear little turrets and gables, and high towers, a long curving wall with dark beams like the peasant cottages, and windows looking out into the forest. It belongs at present to the Grand duke of Sachsen-Weimar-Eisenach.

The Dragon's Tail

Every stone and corner of the Wartburg is connected with some old story or legend.

For instance, there is the hall with the raised dais at one end and beautiful pillars supporting the roof where minnesingers of old times used to hold their great 'musical festivals' as we should say nowadays. There was keen competition for the prizes that were offered in reward for the best music and songs.

In the castle are also the rooms of St Elizabeth, that sweet saint who was so good to the poor, and who suffered so terribly herself in parting from her husband and children.

Then there is the lion on the roof who could tell a fine tale if he chose; the great banqueting hall and the little chapel.

On the top of the tower is a beautiful cross that is lit up at night by electric light and can be seen from a great distance in the country round. This is of course a modern addition.

But the most interesting room in the castle is that where Dr Martin Luther spent his time translating the Bible. A reward had been offered to anyone who should kill this arch-heretic; so his friends brought him disguised as a knight to the Wartburg, and very few people knew of his whereabouts.

As you look through the latticed windows of that little room, the exquisite blue and purple hills of the Thüringen-Wald stretch away in the distance, and no human habitation is to be seen. There too you may see the famous spot on the wall where Luther threw the inkpot at the devil. To be precise, you can see the hole where the ink stain used to be;

for visitors have cut away every trace of the ink, and even portions of the old wooden bedstead. There is the writing desk with the translation of the Bible, and the remarkable footstool that consisted of the bone of a mammoth.

Those were the days in which a man risked his life for his faith; but they were the days also, we must remember, of witchcraft and magic.

One other story of the Wartburg I must narrate in order to give you some idea of the interest that still surrounds the place, and influences the children who grow up there. It was in the days of the old Emperor Barbarossa (Redbeard).

The sister of the Emperor whose name was Jutta, was married to the Landgraf Ludwig of Thüringen, and they lived at the Wartburg.

One day when Barbarossa came to visit them, he observed that the castle had no outer walls round it, as was usual in those days.

'What a pity,' he said, 'that such a fine castle should be unprotected by walls and ramparts. It ought to be more strongly fortified.'

'Oh,' said Landgraf Ludwig, 'if that is all the castle needs, it can soon have them.'

'How soon?' said the Emperor, mockingly.

'In the space of three days,' answered his brother-in-law. 'That could only be possible with the aid of the devil,' said Barbarossa, 'otherwise it could not be done.'

'Wait and see for yourself,' said the Landgraf.

The Dragon's Tail

On the third day of his visit, Ludwig said to the Emperor: 'Would you care to see the walls? They are finished now.' Barbarossa crossed himself several times, and prepared for some fearful manifestation of black magic; but what was his surprise to see a living wall round the castle of stout peasants and burghers, ready armed, with weapons in their hands; the banners of well-known knights and lords waved their pennants in the wind where battlements should have been.

The Emperor was much astonished, and called out: 'Many thanks, brother-in-law, for your lesson; stronger walls I have never seen, nor better fitted together.'

'Rough stones they may some of them be,' said the Landgraf, 'yet I can rely on them, as you see.'

Now as you may imagine, the children who grow up in this town, must have their heads full of these tales, and many poets and artists have been inspired by the beauties of Eisenach. The natural surroundings of the town are so wonderful, that they also provide rich material for the imagination.

Helmut was a boy who lived in Eisenach. He was eight years old, and went to a day school. He lived outside the town, not far from the entrance to the forest. He was a pale, fair-haired little boy, and did not look the tremendous hero he fancied himself in his dreams; not even when he buckled on helmet, breastplate and sword, and marched out into the street to take his part in the warfare that went on constantly there, between the boys of this neighbourhood, and the boys who belonged to another part of the town.

Now the Dragon's Gorge is a most marvellous place; it is surrounded on all sides by thick forests, and you come on it suddenly when walking in the woods. It is a group of huge green rocks like cliffs that stand picturesquely piled close together, towering up to the sky. There is only a very narrow pathway between them.

Helmut had often been there with his father and mother or with other boys. After heavy rain or thawing snow it became impassable; at the best of times it was advisable for a lady not to put on her Sunday hat, especially if it were large and had feathers; for the rocks are constantly dripping with water. The great boulders are covered with green moss or tiny ferns; and in the spring time, wood sorrel grows on them in great patches, the under side of the leaves tinged an exquisite violet or pink colour.

The entrance to the Dragon's Gorge is through these rocks; they narrow and almost meet overhead, obscuring the sky, till it seems as if one were walking under the sea. Two persons cannot walk side by side here. In some parts, indeed, one can only just squeeze through; the way winds in and out in the most curious manner; there are little side passages too, that you could hardly get into at all.

In some places you can hear the water roaring under your feet; then the rocks end abruptly and you come out into the forest again, and hear the birds singing and see the little brook dancing along by the side of the way. Altogether it is the most fascinating, wet and delightful walk that you could imagine.

The Dragon's Tail

Helmut had long been planning an expedition to these rocks in company with other boy friends, in order to slay the dragon. He dreamt of it day and night, until he brought home a bad mark for 'attention' in his school report. He told his mother about it; she laughed and said he might leave the poor old fellow alone; there were plenty of dragons to slay at home, self-will, disobedience, inattention, and so on! She made a momentary impression on the little boy, who always wanted to be good but found it difficult at times, curious to say, to carry out his intention.

He looked thoughtful and answered: 'Of course, mother, I know; but this time I want to slay a 'really and truly' dragon, may I? Will you let me go with the other boys, it would be such fun?'

The Dragon's Gorge was not far off, and mother did not think that Helmut could do himself any harm, except by getting wet and dirty, and that he might do as well in the garden at home.

'If you put on your old suit and your thick boots, I think you may go. Keep with the other boys, and promise me not to get lost!'

'Oh, I say, won't it be fine fun! I'll run off and tell the other fellows. Hurrah!' and Helmut ran off into the street. Soon four heads were to be seen close together making plans for the next day.

'We'll start quite early at six o'clock,' they said, 'and take our second breakfast together.' (In Germany, the eleven o'clock lunch is called second breakfast.) However, it was seven o'clock before the boys had had their first breakfast, and met outside the house.

How mother and father laughed to see the little fellows, all dressed in the most warlike costumes like miniature soldiers, armed with guns and swords.

Mother was a little anxious and hoped they would come to no harm; but she liked her boy to be independent, and knew how happy children are if left to play their pretence games alone. She watched the four set off at a swinging march down the street. Soon they had recruits, for it was a holiday, and there were plenty of boys about.

Helmut was the commanding officer; the boys shouldered their guns, or presented arms as he directed. They passed the pond and followed the stream through the woods, until they came to the Dragon's Gorge, where the rocks rise up suddenly high and imposing looking. Here they could only proceed in single file.

Helmut headed the band feeling as courageous as in his dreams; his head swam with elation. Huge walls towered above them; the rocks dropped water on their heads. As yet they had seen or heard nothing of the dragon. Yet as they held their breath to listen, they could hear something roaring under their feet.

'Don't you tell me that that is only water,' said Helmut, 'A little brook can't make such a row as that—that's the dragon.' The other boys laughed, they were sceptical as to the dragon, and were only pretending, whereas Helmut was in earnest. 'I'm hungry,' said one boy, 'supposing we find a dry place and have our lunch!'

They came to where the path wound out again into the open air, and sat down on some stones, which could hardly be described as dry. Here they ate bread and sausage, oranges and bananas.

'Give me the orange peel, you fellows. Mother hates us to throw it about; it makes the place so untidy.' So saying Helmut pushed his orange peel right into a crevice of the rock and covered it with old leaves. But the other boys laughed at him, and chucked theirs into the little stream, which made Helmut very angry.

'I won't be your officer any more, if you do not do as I say,' he said, and they began to quarrel.

'We're not going to fight your old dragon, we're going home again to play football, that will be far better fun,' said the boys who had joined as recruits, and they went off home, till only Helmut's chums were left. They were glad enough to get rid of the other boys.

'We have more chance of seeing the dragon without those stupid fellows,' they said.

They finished their lunch, shouldered their guns again, and entered the second gorge, which is even more picturesque and narrow than the first.

Suddenly Helmut espied something round, and slimy, and long lying on the path before him like a blind worm, but much thicker than blind worms generally are. He became fearfully excited, 'Come along you fellows, hurry up,' he said, 'I do believe it is the dragon's tail!'

They came up close behind him and looked over his shoulders; the gorge was so narrow here that they could not pass one another.

'Good gracious!' they said, 'whatever shall we do now?' They all felt frightened at the idea of a real dragon, but they stood to their guns like men, all but the youngest, Adolf, who wanted to run away home; but the others would not let him. 'Helmut catch hold of it, quick now,' whispered Werner and Wolf, the other two boys.

Helmut stretched out his hand courageously; perhaps it was only a huge, blind worm after all; but as he tried to catch it, the thing slipped swiftly away. They all followed it, running as fast as they could through the narrow gorge, bumping themselves against the walls, scratching themselves and tearing their clothes, but all the time Helmut never let that tail (if it was a tail) out of his sight.

'If we had some salt to put on it,' said he, 'we might catch it like a dicky bird.'

'It would be a fine thing to present to a museum,' said Wolf.

Well, that thing led them a fine dance. It would stop short, and then when they thought they had got it, it started off again, until they were all puffing and blowing.

'We've got to catch it somehow,' said Helmut, who

thought the chase to be a fine sport. At that moment the gorge opened out again into the woods, and the tail gave them the slip; for it disappeared in a crevice of the rock where there was no room for a boy to follow it.

'It was a blind worm you see,' said Werner.

Presently, however, they heard a noise as of thunder, and looking down the path they saw a head glaring at them out of the rocks, undeniably a dragon's head, with a huge jaw, red tongue, and rows of jagged teeth.

The boys stared aghast: they were in for an adventure this time, and no mistake. Slowly the dragon raised himself out of the rocks, so that they saw his whole scaly length, like a huge crocodile. Then he began to move along the path away from them. He moved quite slowly now, so there was no difficulty in keeping up with him; but his tail was so slimy and slippery that they could not keep hold of it; moreover it wriggled dreadfully whenever they tried to seize it. But Helmut had inherited the cool courage of the Wartburg knights, and he was not going to be overcome by difficulties.

With a wild Indian whoop he sprang on the dragon's back, and all the other boys followed his example, except little Adolf who was timid and began to set up a howl for his mother. No sooner were the boys on his back than the dragon set off at a fine trot up and down the Dragon's Gorge, they had to hold on tight and to duck whenever the rock projected overhead, or when they went sharply round a corner.

'Hurrah!' cried Helmut waving a flag, 'This is better than a motor ride. Isn't he a jolly old fellow?'

At this remark the jolly old fellow stopped dead, and began to snort out fire and smoke, that made the boys cough and choke.

'Now stop that, will you!' said Helmut imperatively, 'or we shall have to slay you after all, that's what we came out for you know.' He pointed his gun at the head of the dragon as he spoke like a real hero.

The dragon began to tremble, and though they could only see his profile, they thought he turned pale.

'Where's that other little boy?' he asked in a hollow voice. 'If you will give him to me for my dinner, I will spare you all.' Helmut laughed scornfully, 'Thanks, old fellow,' he said, 'you're very kind. I'm sure Adolf would be much obliged to you. I expect he's run home to his mother long ago; he's a bit of a funk, we shan't take him with us another time.'

'He looked so sweet and juicy and tender,' said the dragon sighing, 'I never get a child for dinner nowadays! Woe is me,' he sniffed.

'You are an old cannibal,' said the boys horrified, and mistaking the meaning of the word cannibal. 'Hurry up now and give us another ride, it's first-rate fun!'

The dragon groaned and seemed disinclined to stir, but the boys kicked him with their heels, and there was nothing for it but to gee up.

After he had been up and down several times, and the

boys' clothes were nearly torn to pieces, he suddenly turned into a great crevice in the rocks that led down into a dark passage, and the boys felt really frightened for the first time. Daylight has a wonderfully bracing effect on the nerves.

In a moment, however, a few rays of sunshine penetrated the black darkness, and they saw that they were in a small cave. The next thing they experienced was that the dragon shook himself violently, and the small boys fell off his back like apples from a tree on to the wet and sloppy floor. They picked themselves up again in a second, and there they saw the dragon before them, panting after his exertions and filling the cavern with a poisonous-smelling smoke.

Helmut and Wolf and Werner stood near the cracks which did the duty of windows, and held their pistols pointed at him. Luckily, he was too stupid to know that they were only toy guns, and when they fired them off crack-crack, they soon discovered that he was in a terrible fright.

'What have I done to you, young sirs?' he gasped out. 'What have I done to you, that you should want to shoot me? Yet shoot me! Yes, destroy me if you will and end my miserable existence!' He began to groan until the cavern reverberated with his cries.

'What's the matter now, old chappie?' said Helmut, who, observing the weakness of the enemy, had regained his courage. 'I am an anachronism,' said the dragon, 'don't you know what that is?—well, I am one born out of my age. I am a survival of anything but the fittest. You are the masters now, you miserable floppy-looking race of mankind. You can shoot me, you can blow me up with dynamite, you can poison me, you can stuff me—Oh, oh—you can put me into a cage in the Zoological Gardens, you have flying dragons in the sky who could drop on me suddenly and crush me. You have the power. We great creatures of bygone ages have only been able to creep into the rocks and caves to hide from your superior cleverness and your wily machinations. We must perish while you go on like the brook for ever.' So saying he began to shed great tears, that dropped on the floor splash-splash like the water from the rocks.

The boys felt embarrassed: this was not their idea of manly conduct, and considerably lowered their opinion of dragons in general.

'Do not betray me, young sirs,' went on the dragon in a pathetic and weepy voice, 'I have managed so far to lie here concealed though multitudes of people have passed this way and never perceived me.'

'I tell you what,' said Helmut touched by the dragon's evident terror, 'let's make friends with him, boys; he's given us a nice ride for nothing; we will present him with the flag of truce.'

Turning to the dragon he said: 'Allow us to give you a banana and a roll in token of our friendship and esteem.'

'Oh!' said the dragon brightening up, 'I like bananas. People often throw the skins away here. I prefer them to orange peel. I live on such things, you must know, the cast-off refuse of humanity,' he said, becoming tragic again.

They presented him with the banana, and he ate it skin and all, it seemed to give him an appetite. He appeared to recover his spirits, and the boys thought it would be better to look for the way out.

The cavern seemed quite smooth and round, except for the cracks through which the daylight came; they could not discover the passage by which they had entered. The dragon's eyes were beginning to look bloodthirsty; remembrances of his former strength shot across his dulled brains. He could crush and eat these little boys after all and nobody would be the wiser. Little boys tasted nicer than bananas even.

Meanwhile, Wolf and Werner had stuck their flags through the holes in the rocks, so that they were visible from the outside.

Now little Adolf had gone straight home, and had told awful tales of the games the others were up to, and he conducted the four mothers to the Dragon's Gorge where they wandered up and down looking for their boys. Adolf observed the flags sticking up on the rocks, and drew attention to them. The Dragon's Gorge resounded with the cries of 'Helmut! Wolf! Werner!'

The dragon heard the voices as well; his evil intentions died away; the chronic fear of discovery dawned upon him again. He grew paler and paler; clouds of smoke came from his nostrils, until he became invisible. At the same moment, Helmut, groping against the wall that lay in shadow, found the opening of the passage through which they had come. Through this the three boys now crawled, hardly daring to breathe, for fear of exciting the dragon again. Soon a gleam of light at the other end told of their deliverance. Their tender mothers fell on their necks, and scolded them at the same time. Truly, never did boys look dirtier or more disreputable.

'We feel positively ashamed to go home with you,' their mothers said to them.

'Well, for once I was jolly glad you did come, mother,' said Helmut. 'That treacherous old dragon wanted to turn on us after all; he might have devoured us, if you had not turned up in the nick of time. Not that I believe that he really would have done anything of the sort, he was a coward you know, and when we levelled our guns at him he was awfully frightened. Still he might have found out that our guns were not properly loaded, and then it would have been unpleasant.'

Mother smiled, she did not seem to take the story quite so seriously as Helmut wished.

'We had a gorgeous ride on his back, mother dear; would you like to see him? You have only to lie down flat and squeeze yourself through that crack in the rocks till you come to his cave.'

'No, thank you,' said mother, 'I think I can do without seeing your dragon.'

'Oh, we have forgotten our flags!' called out Wolf and Werner, 'Wait a minute for us,' and they climbed up over the rocks and rescued the flags. 'He's still in there,' they whispered to Helmut in a mysterious whisper.

'Mother,' said Helmut that evening when she came to wish him good night, 'do you know, if you stand up to a dragon like a man, and are not afraid of him, he is not so difficult to vanquish after all.'

'I'm glad you think so,' said mother, '"Volo cum Deo"—there is a Latin proverb for you; it means, that with God's help, will-power is the chief thing necessary; this even dragons know. Thus a little boy can conquer even greater dragons than the monsters vast of ages past.'

'Hum!' said Helmut musingly, 'Mother dear, I was a real hero today, I think you would have been proud of me; but I must confess between ourselves, that the old dragon was a bit of a fool!'

Acknowledgements

This completed work is a synergistic product of many minds.

I thank my husband, Rishi Sehgal, my entire family and all my dear friends for being patient and encouraging.

I bear a deep sense of sincere appreciation for Yamini Chowdhury for her efficient and professional approach to the work. My earnest regards to Aditi Mehrotra for devoting her valuable time and giving editorial inputs, which has helped shape this book. I express my gratitude to the most diligent team of Rupa Publications for their efforts.

To acknowledge is to express my gratitude to all of you who undoubtedly remain an integral part of my extraordinary journey. Your unwavering support and encouragement have truly made this book possible.